MARVEL

THOR
RAGNAROK

MARVEL
marvelkids.com
© 2017 MARVEL

Illustrations by Ron Lim

Cover design by Elaine Lopez-Levine. Cover illustration by Ron Lim.

Little, Brown and Company
Hachette Book Group
1290 Avenue of the Americas, New York, NY 10104
Visit us at LBYR.com
marvelkids.com

First Edition: October 2017

Little, Brown and Company is a division of Hachette Book Group, Inc.
The Little, Brown name and logo are trademarks of Hachette Book Group, Inc.

The publisher is not responsible for websites (or their content) that are not owned by the publisher.

ISBNs: 978-0-316-41391-6 (pbk.), 978-0-316-41396-1 (ebook), 978-0-316-41394-7 (ebook), 978-0-316-41395-4 (ebook)

Printed in the United States of America

CW

10 9 8 7 6 5 4 3 2 1

MARVEL
THOR
RAGNAROK
GET IN THE RING!

Adapted by R. R. Busse
Illustrations by Ron Lim
Based on the Screenplay by Eric Pearson
Story by Craig Kyle & Christopher Yost and Eric Pearson
Produced by Kevin Feige, p.g.a.
Directed by Taika Waititi

(L B)

LITTLE, BROWN AND COMPANY
New York   Boston

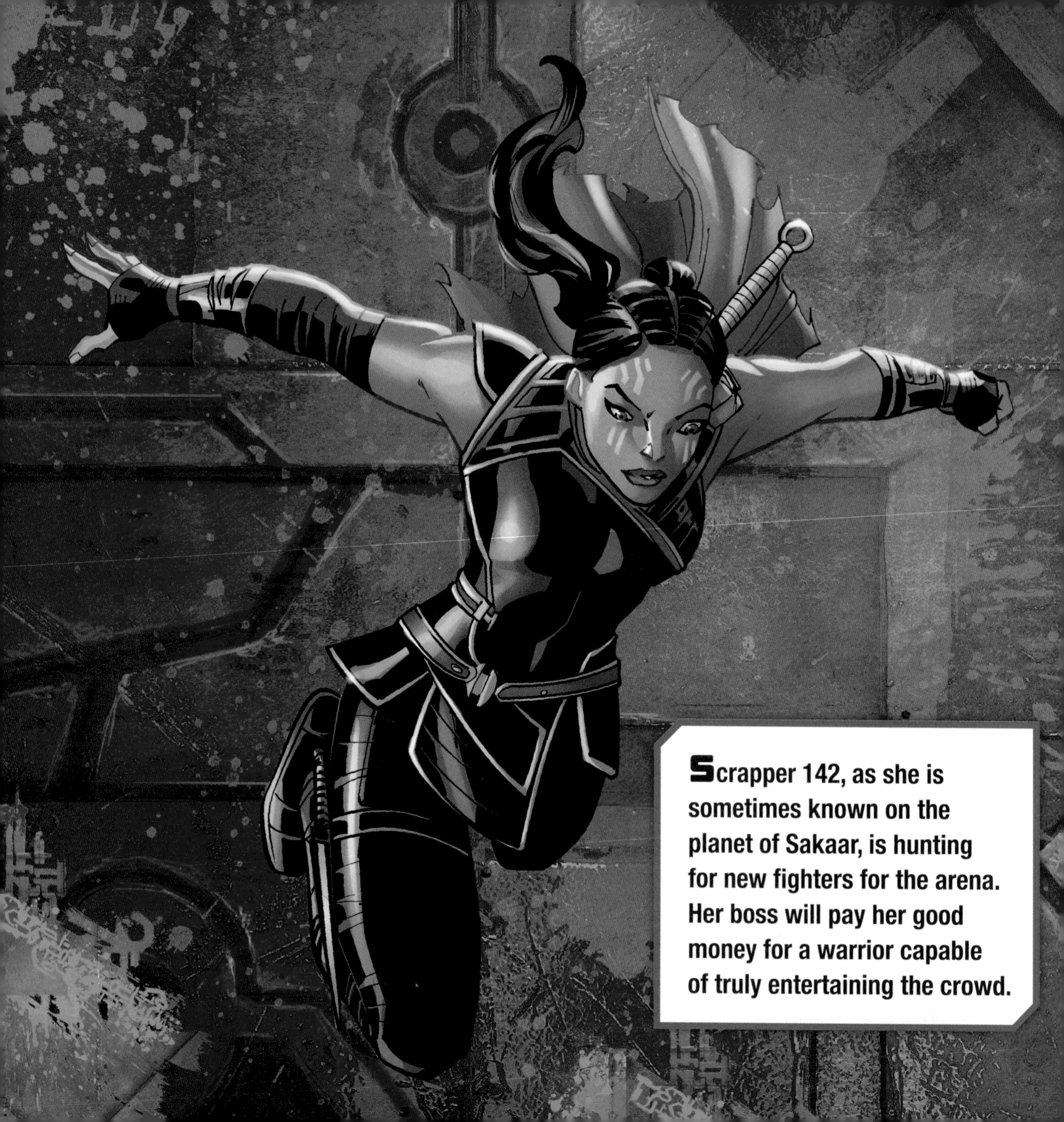

Scrapper 142, as she is sometimes known on the planet of Sakaar, is hunting for new fighters for the arena. Her boss will pay her good money for a warrior capable of truly entertaining the crowd.

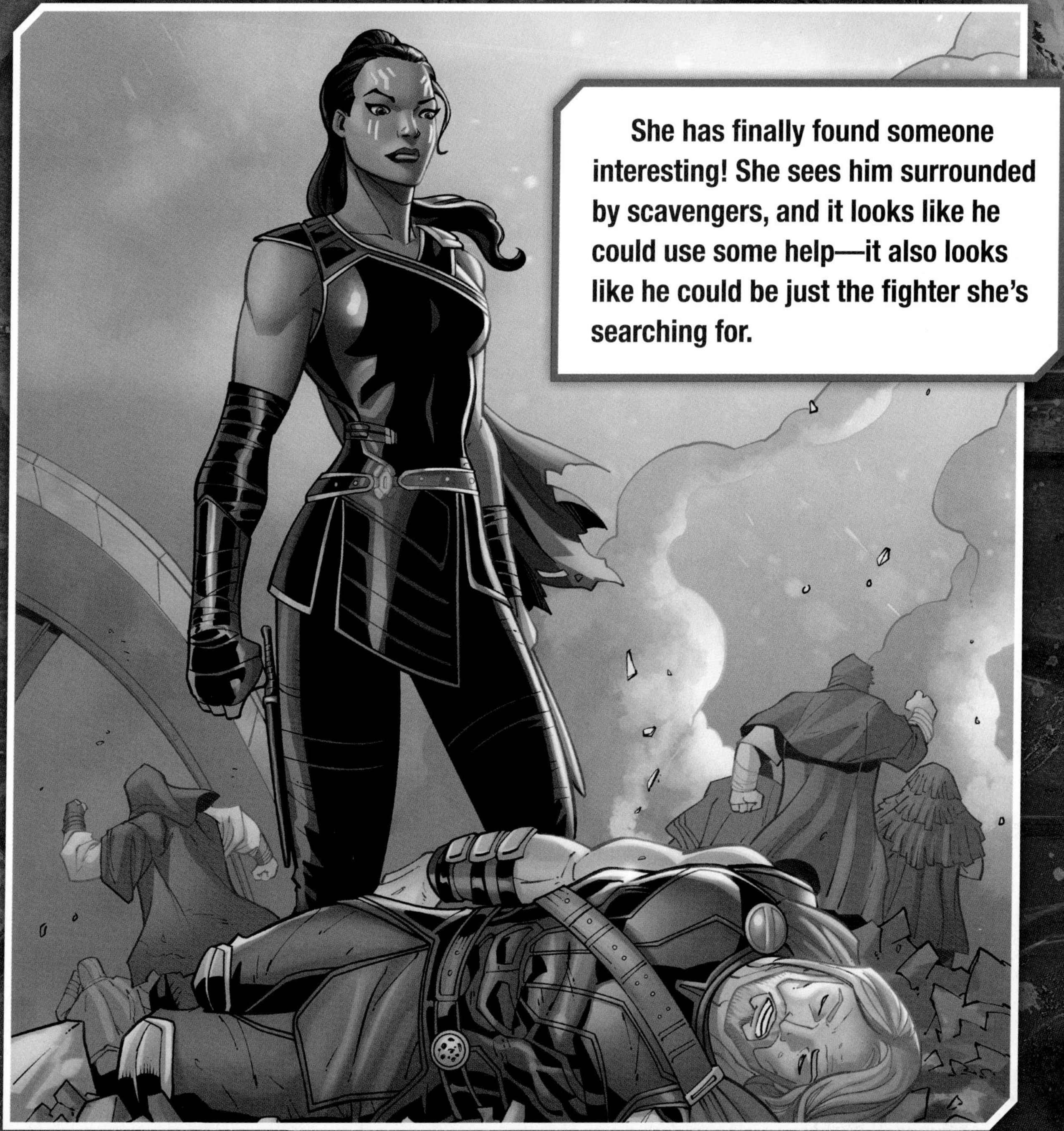

She has finally found someone interesting! She sees him surrounded by scavengers, and it looks like he could use some help—it also looks like he could be just the fighter she's searching for.

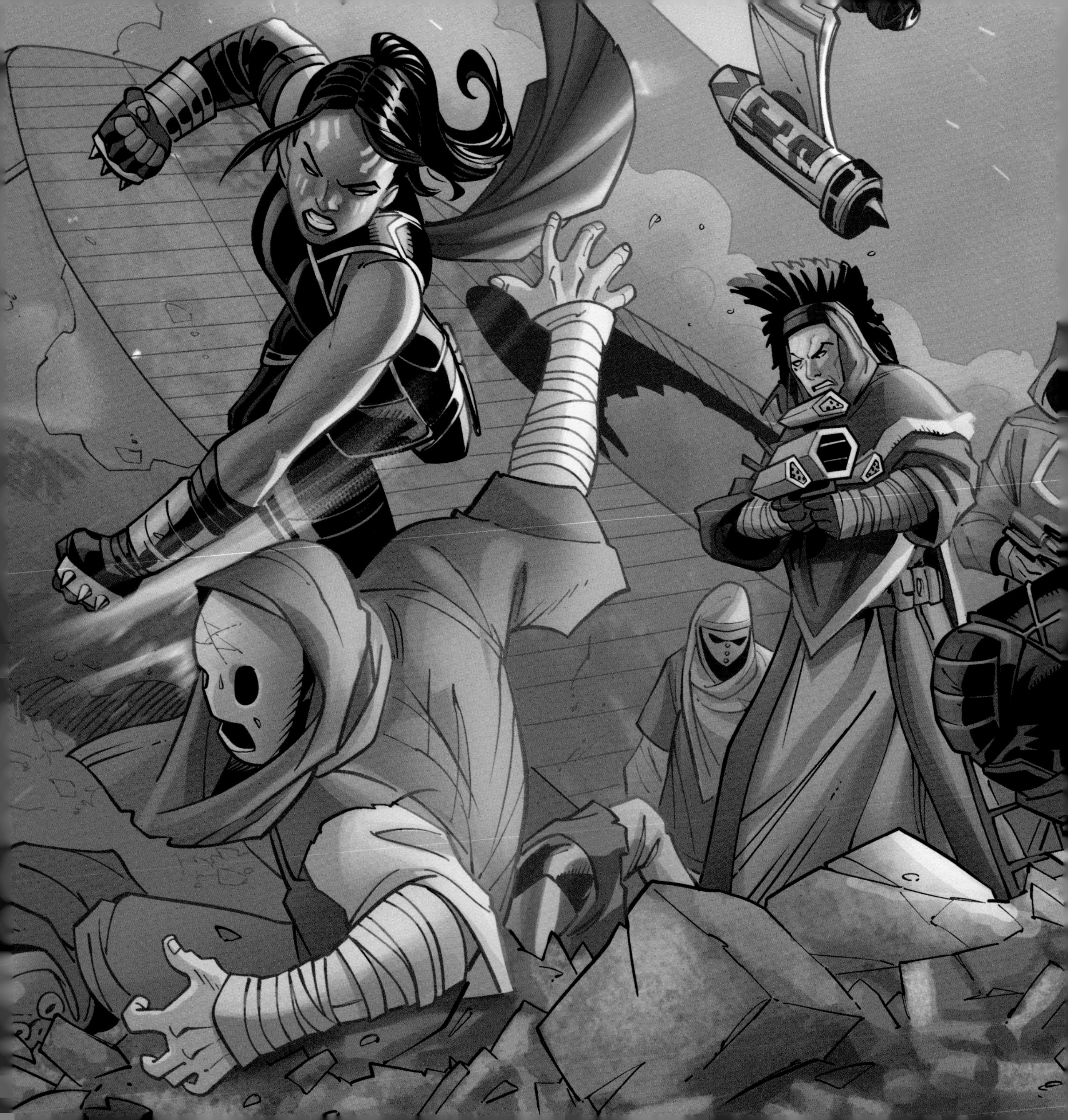

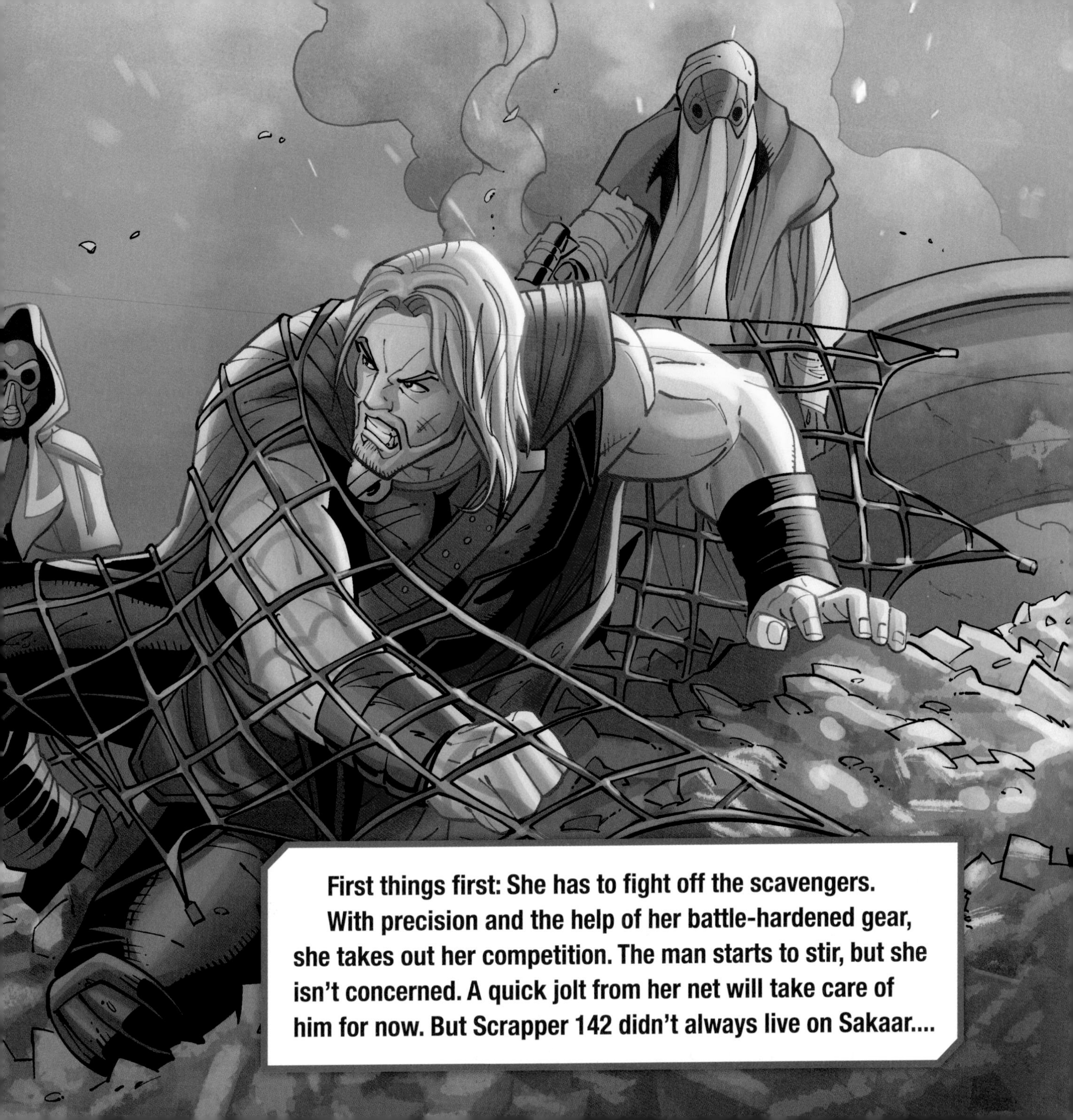

First things first: She has to fight off the scavengers.

With precision and the help of her battle-hardened gear, she takes out her competition. The man starts to stir, but she isn't concerned. A quick jolt from her net will take care of him for now. But Scrapper 142 didn't always live on Sakaar....

VALKYRIE

A tough-as-nails galactic scavenger with a mysterious past. After a tragedy left her life in tatters, Valkyrie disappeared to a corner of the galaxy where she could move on. Now with the universe in peril, she must put her history behind her to save it in its darkest hour.

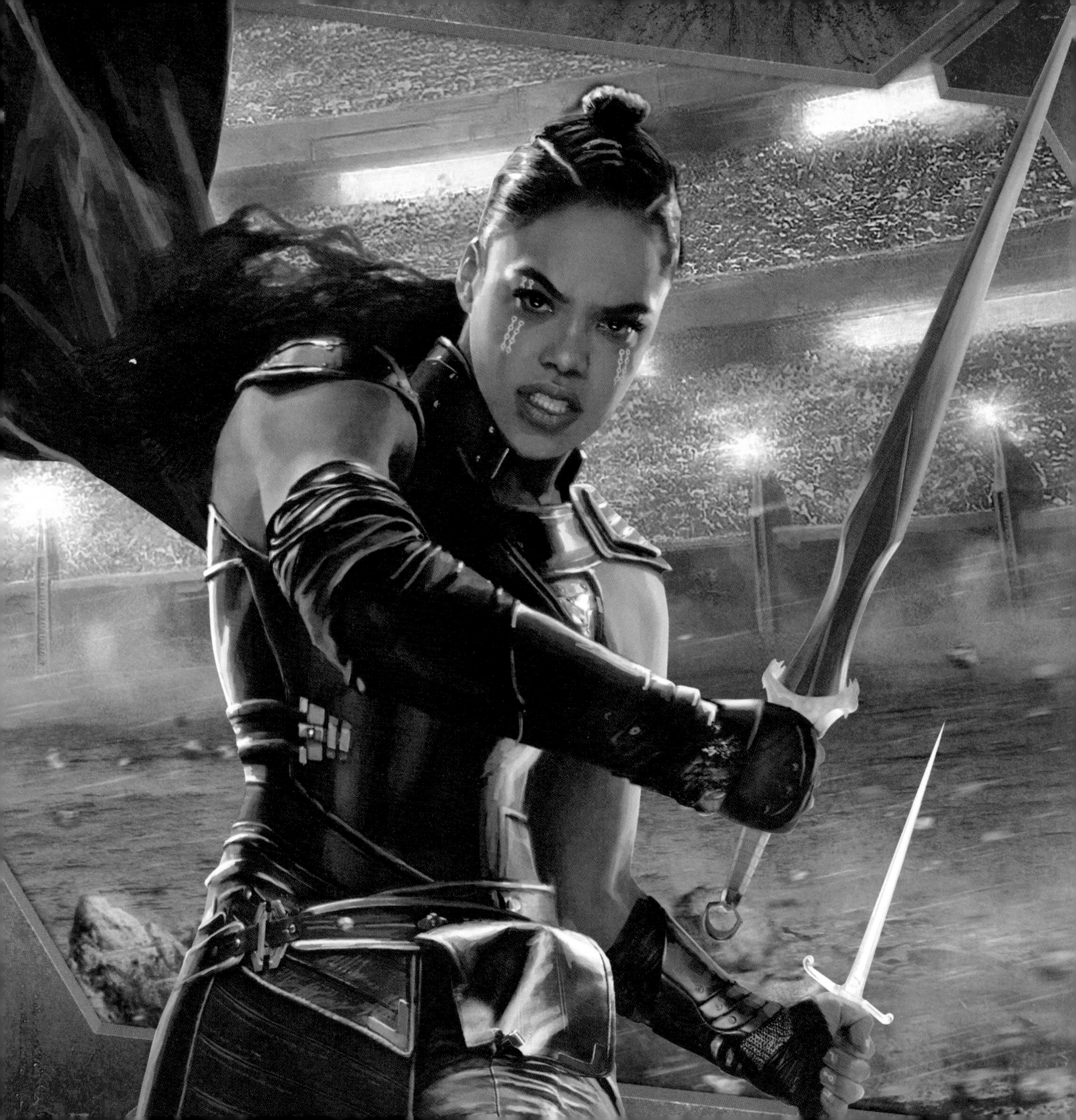

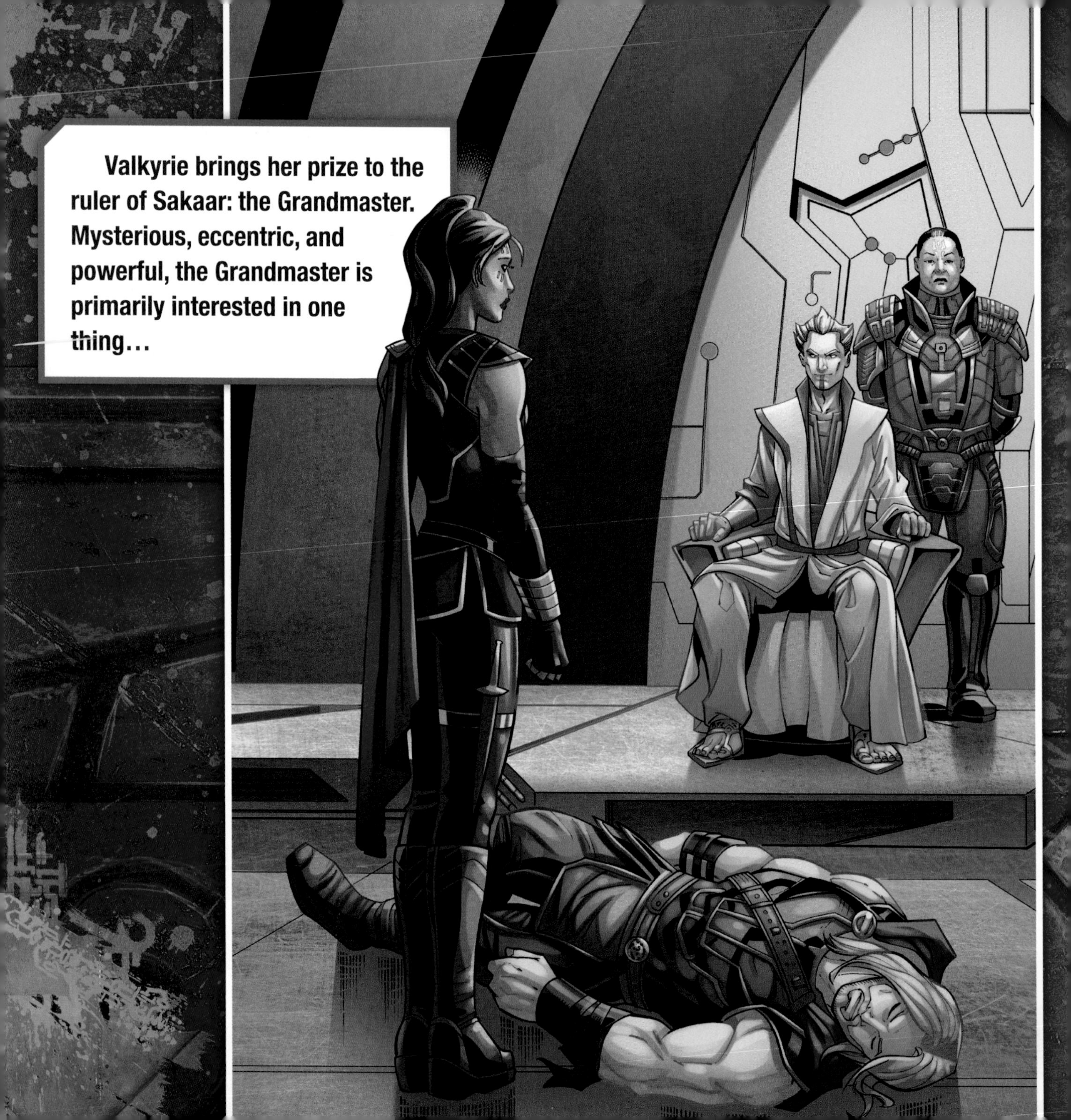
Valkyrie brings her prize to the ruler of Sakaar: the Grandmaster. Mysterious, eccentric, and powerful, the Grandmaster is primarily interested in one thing…

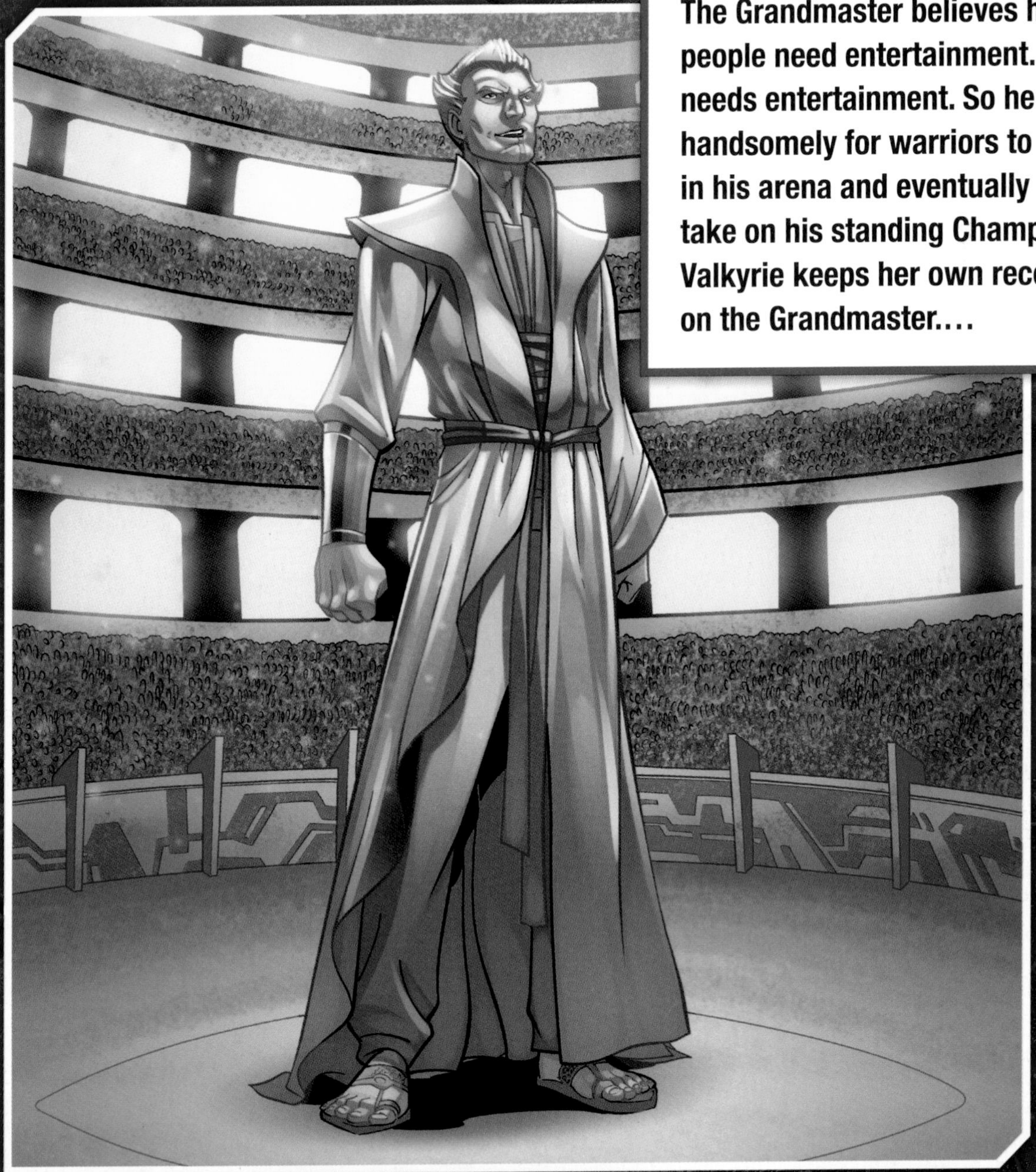

…his Contest of Champions! The Grandmaster believes his people need entertainment. *He* needs entertainment. So he pays handsomely for warriors to fight in his arena and eventually take on his standing Champion. Valkyrie keeps her own record on the Grandmaster.…

THE GRANDMASTER

The exuberant and dangerous ruler of Sakaar, a planet built on chaos and indulgence, the Grandmaster controls an incredible gladiatorial contest in which his Champion and other powerful beings from throughout the cosmos face off in spectacular and deadly combat.

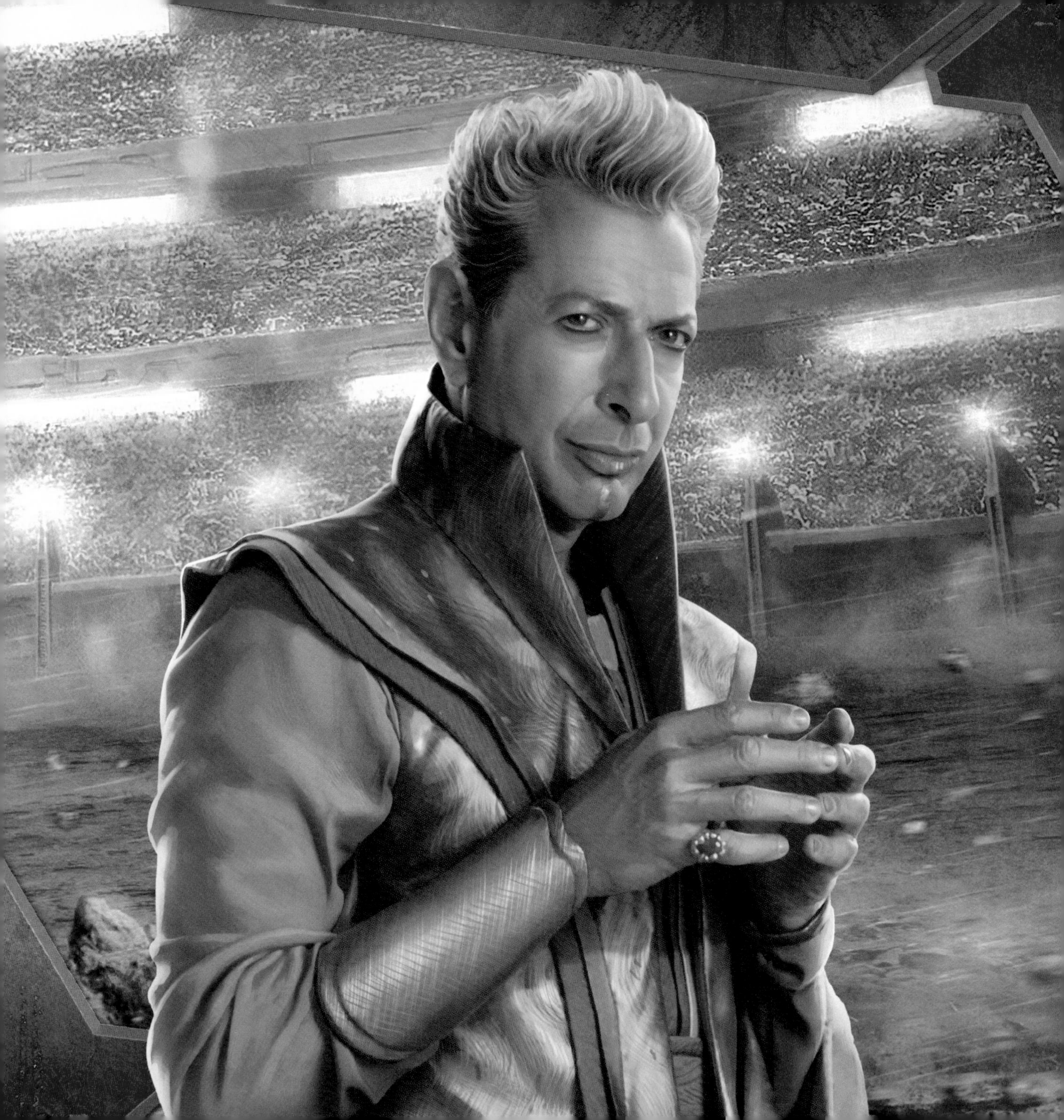

The fighter is worth Valkyrie's effort. While Valkyrie collects her money, the Grandmaster asks the fighter, "Tell me: What's your story? Who are you? Where do you come from?" The Grandmaster sits back, genuine interest in his eyes.

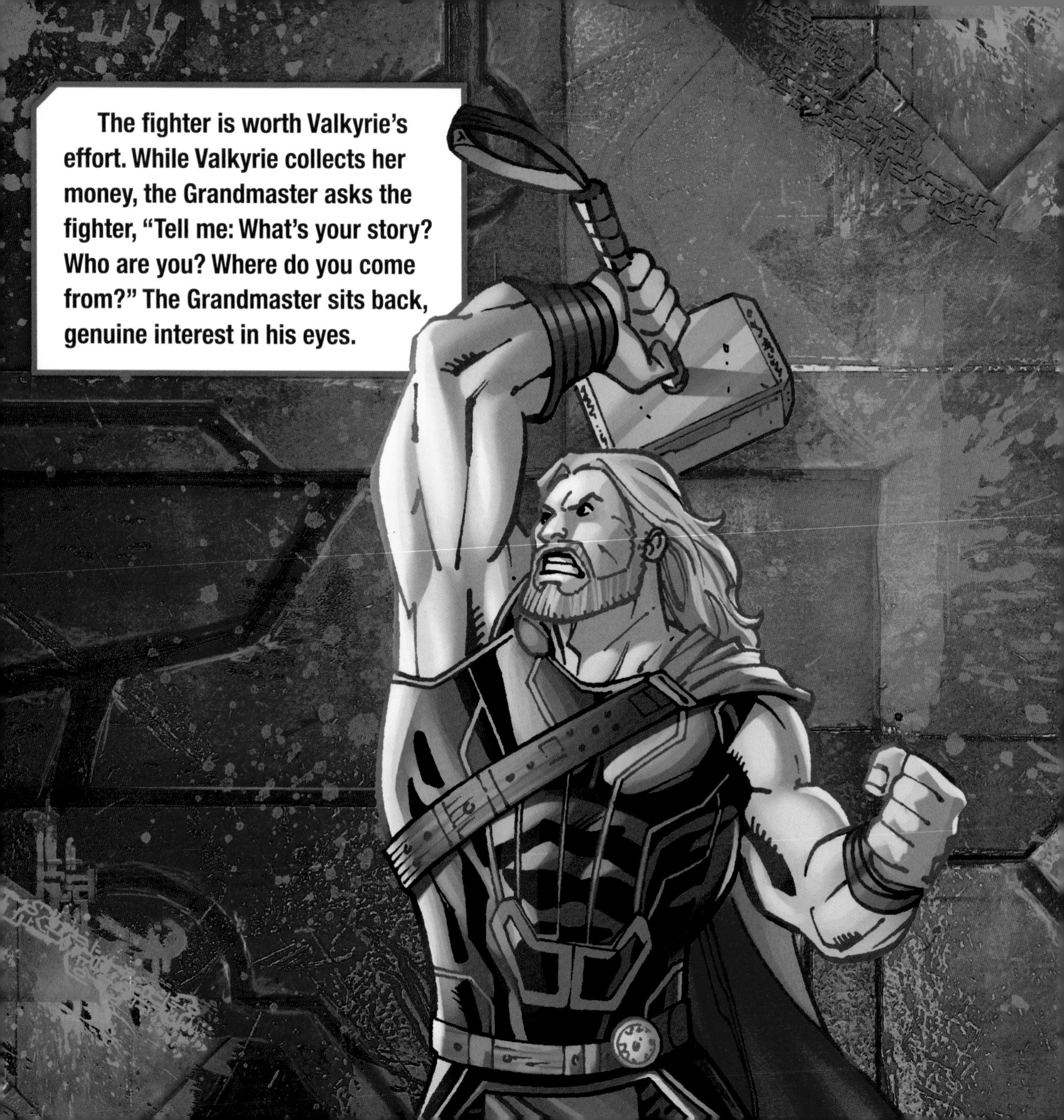

"I am Thor Odinson from Asgard…." Valkyrie's contender says.

Thor—she knows that name. After his conversation with the Grandmaster and preparation from the arena's workers, Thor joins his fellow gladiators.

Valkyrie updates her files on the Asgardian….

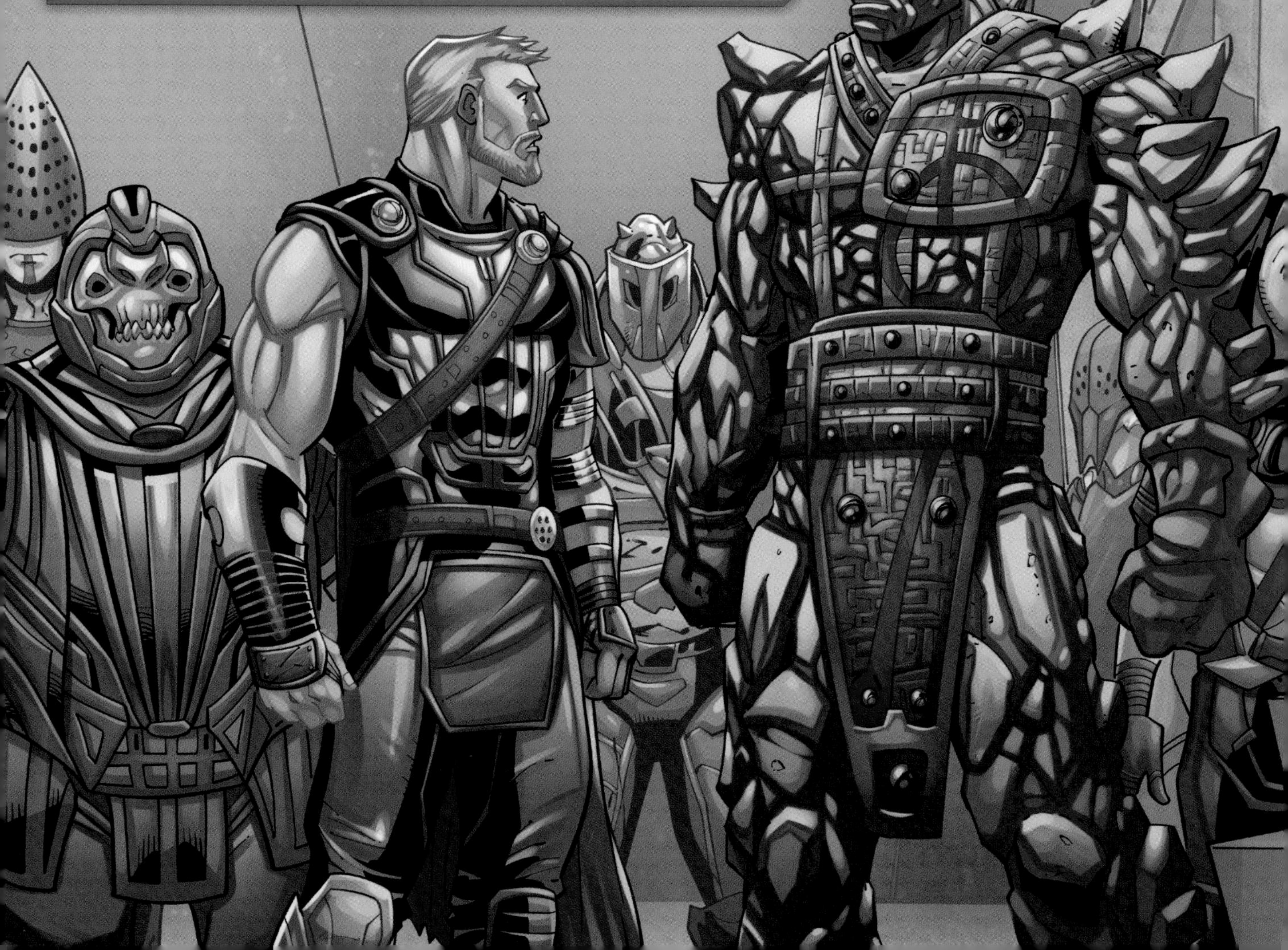

THOR

When an ancient evil, lurking for eons, is released from its shackles, the Asgardian prince of thunder is thrown into a whirlwind of chaos. Ripped from his familiar surroundings and stripped of his powers, Thor's only hope is to summon the warrior within, and fight his way back against impossible odds. With his world shattered, Thor must discover what it means to be a true leader.

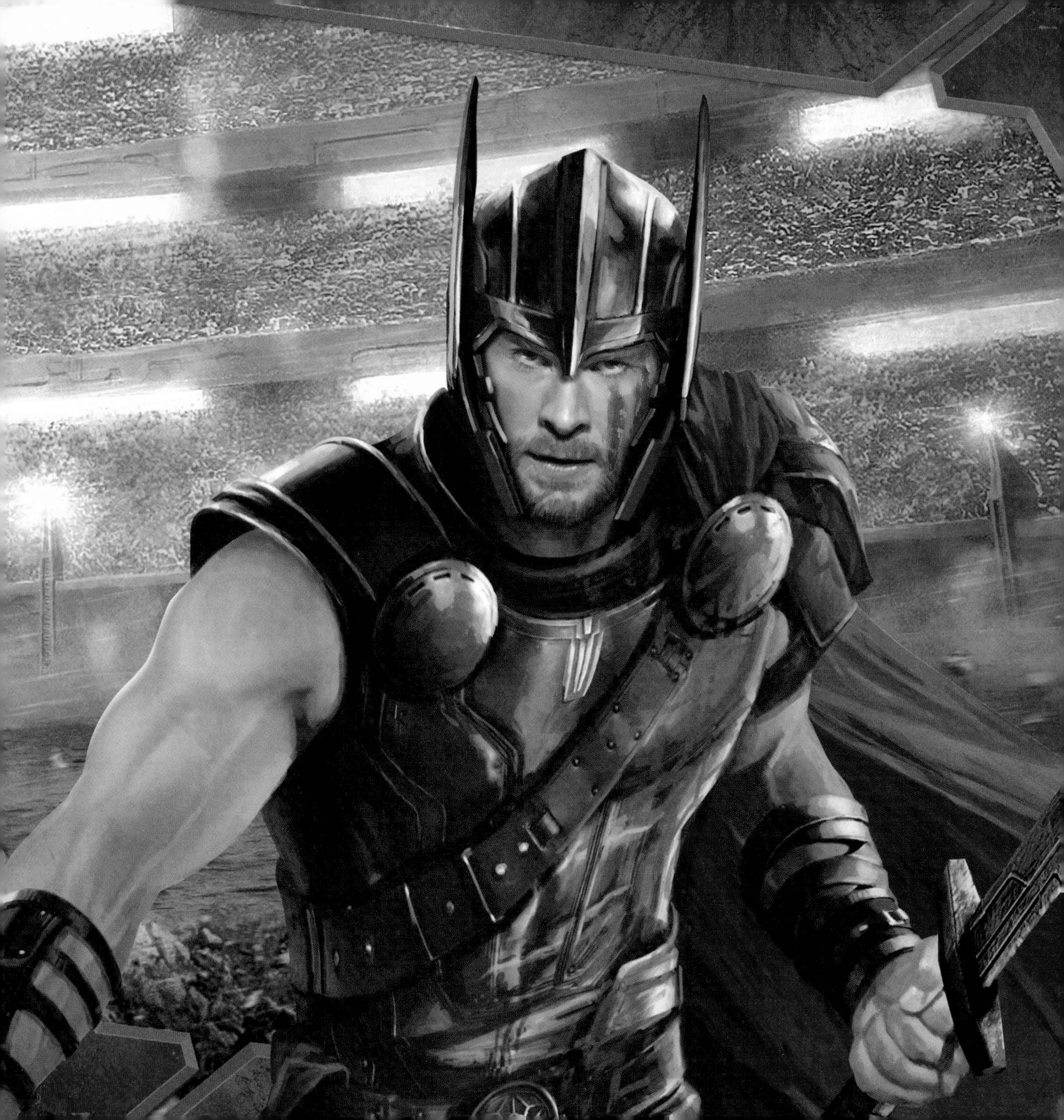

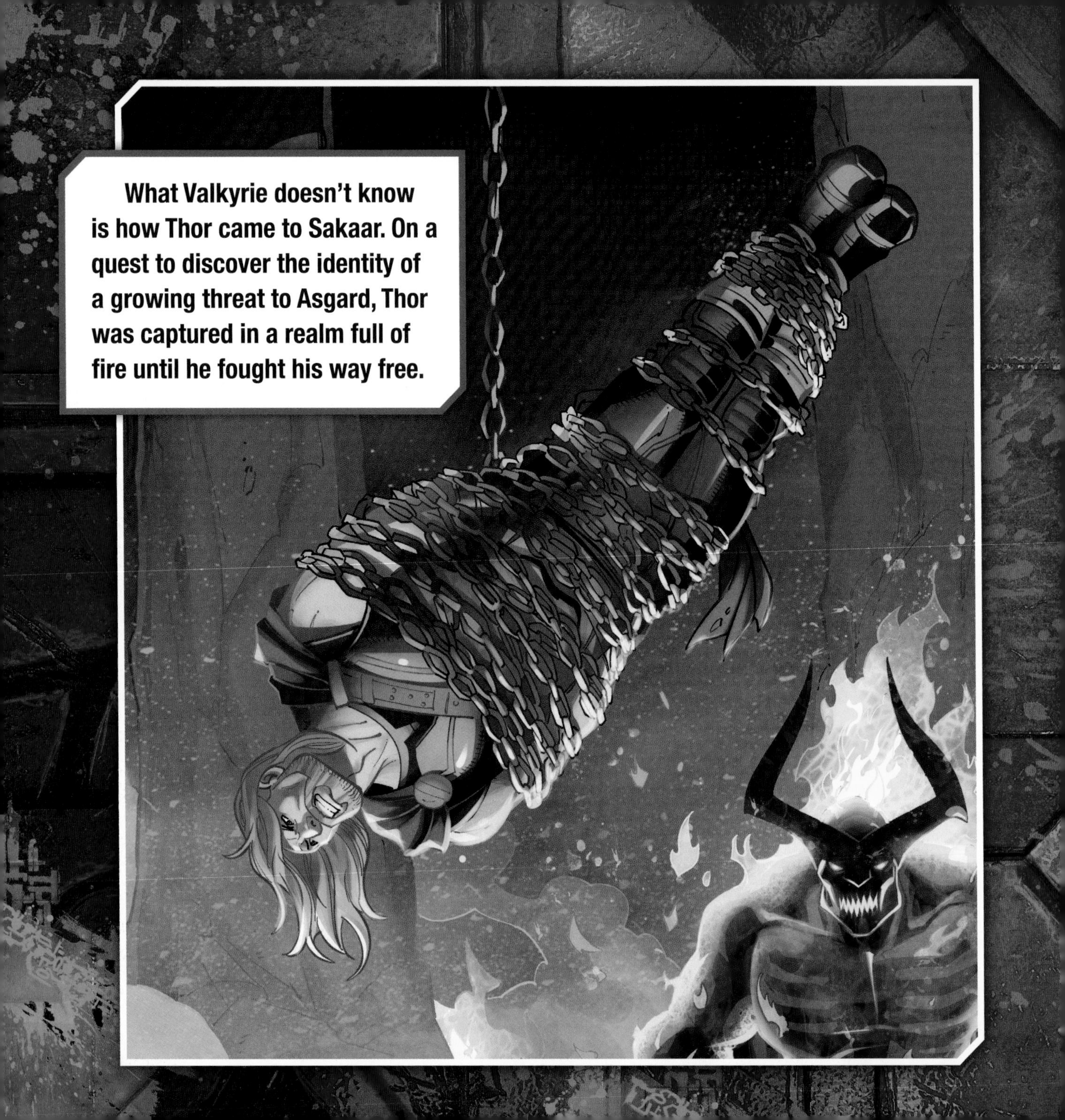
What Valkyrie doesn't know is how Thor came to Sakaar. On a quest to discover the identity of a growing threat to Asgard, Thor was captured in a realm full of fire until he fought his way free.

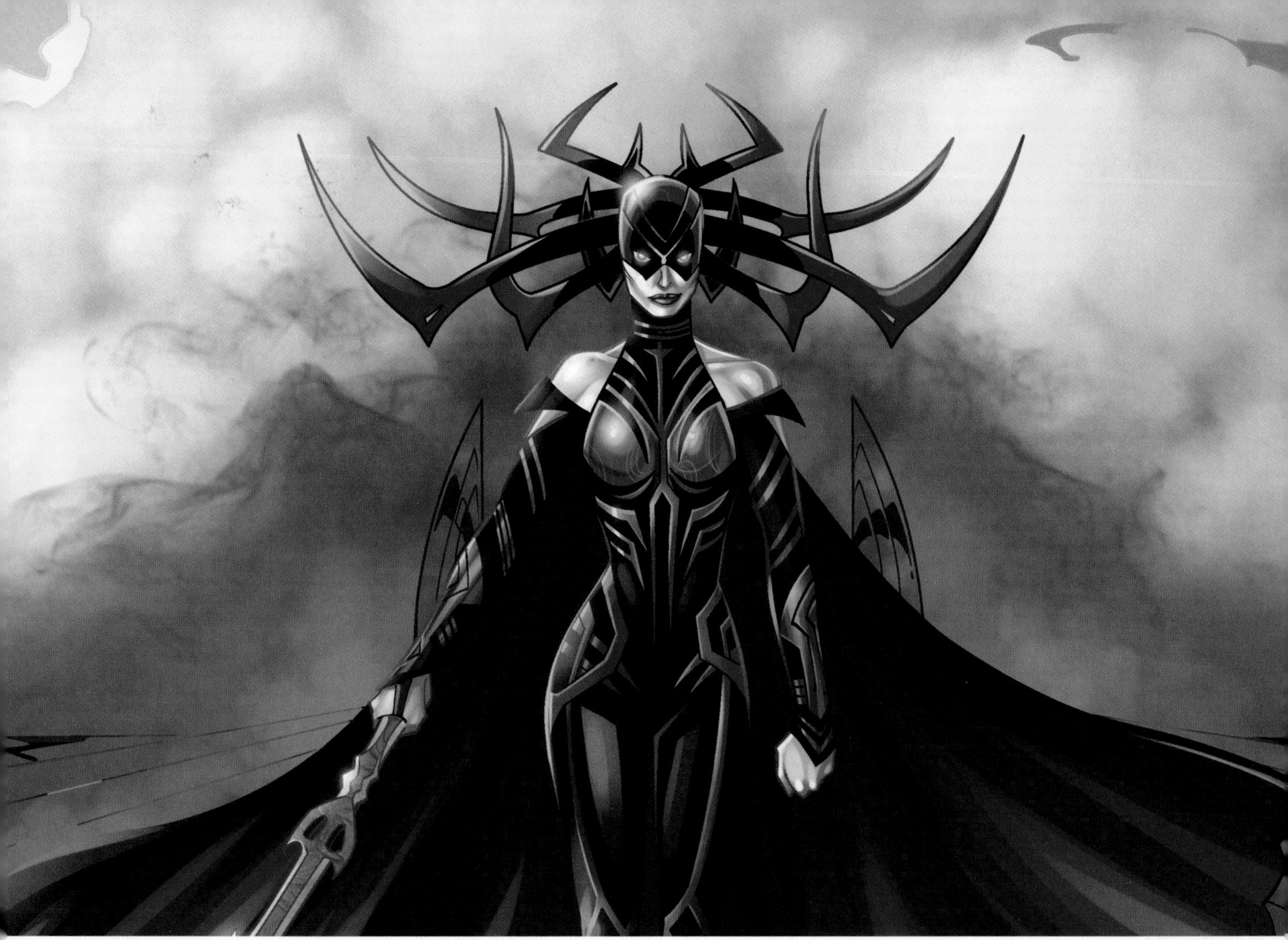

But Hela, an ancient evil with a burning hatred for Asgard, saw what Thor was doing and ambushed him on the Bifrost—the link between realms—and knocked him off course; that's when he landed on Sakaar.

Valkyrie's records on Hela are in need of an update....

HELA

A creature from a primordial and sinister era of the universe, Hela's power is unlike anything else in the Nine Realms. Armed with the ability to unleash unlimited weapons in astounding and deadly ways, Hela seeks vengeance against those who imprisoned her eons ago. She will usher in a new era of cold brutality for Asgard and the universe at large.

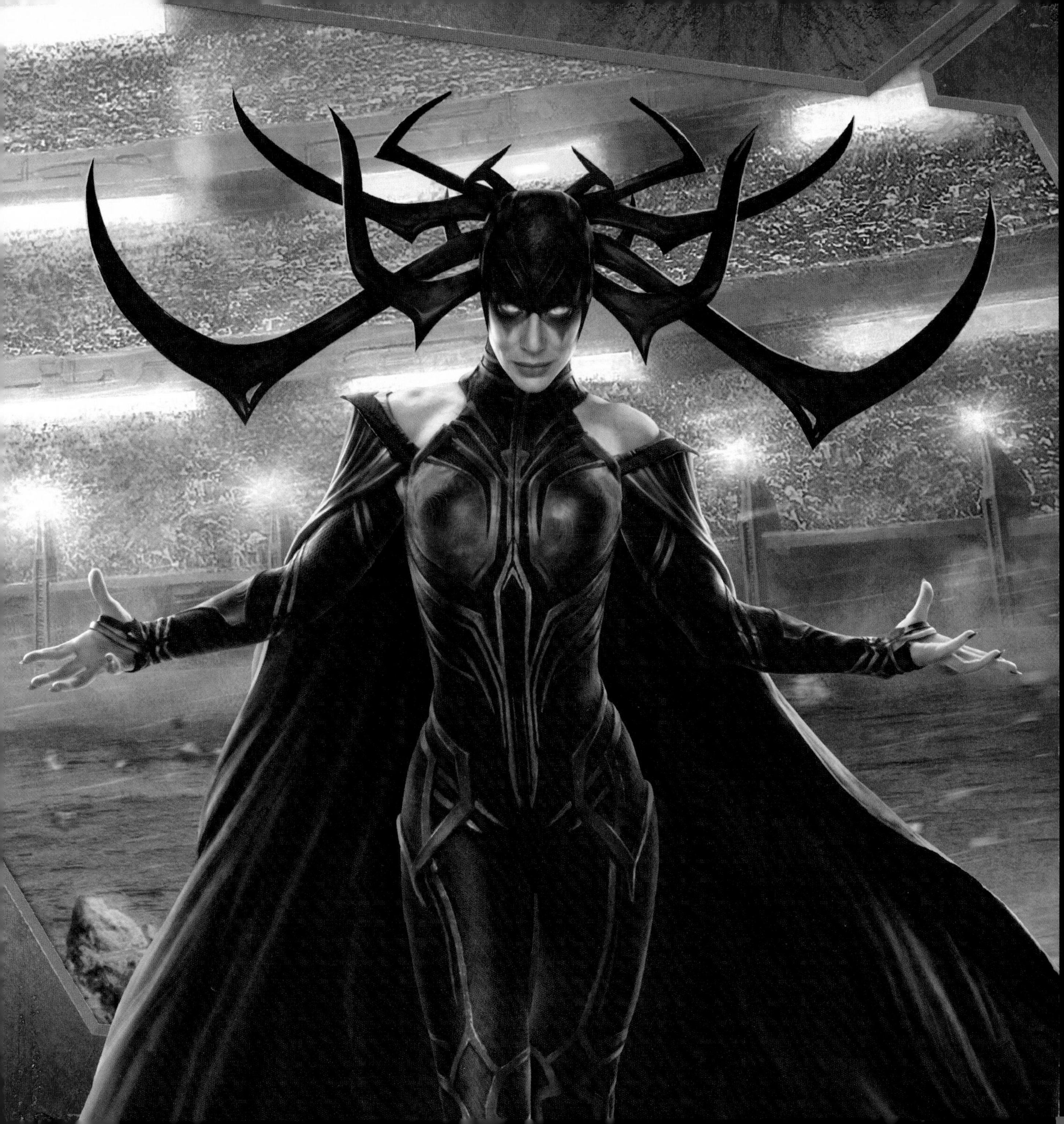

By now, Thor is prepared to take on the Champion. The undefeated green behemoth crushes his enemies with frightening strength and ferocity. The Champion is known simply as…the Incredible Hulk!

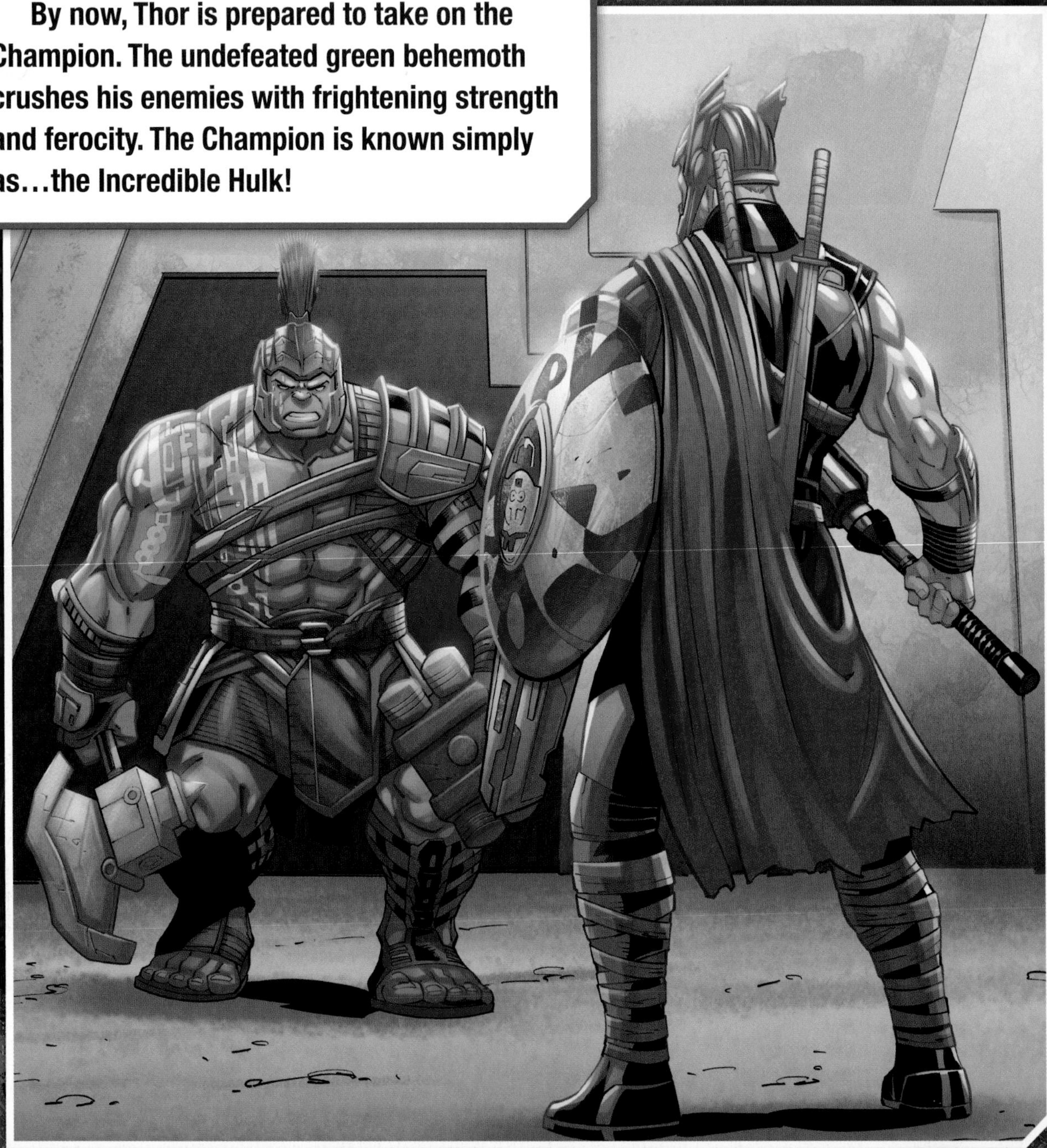

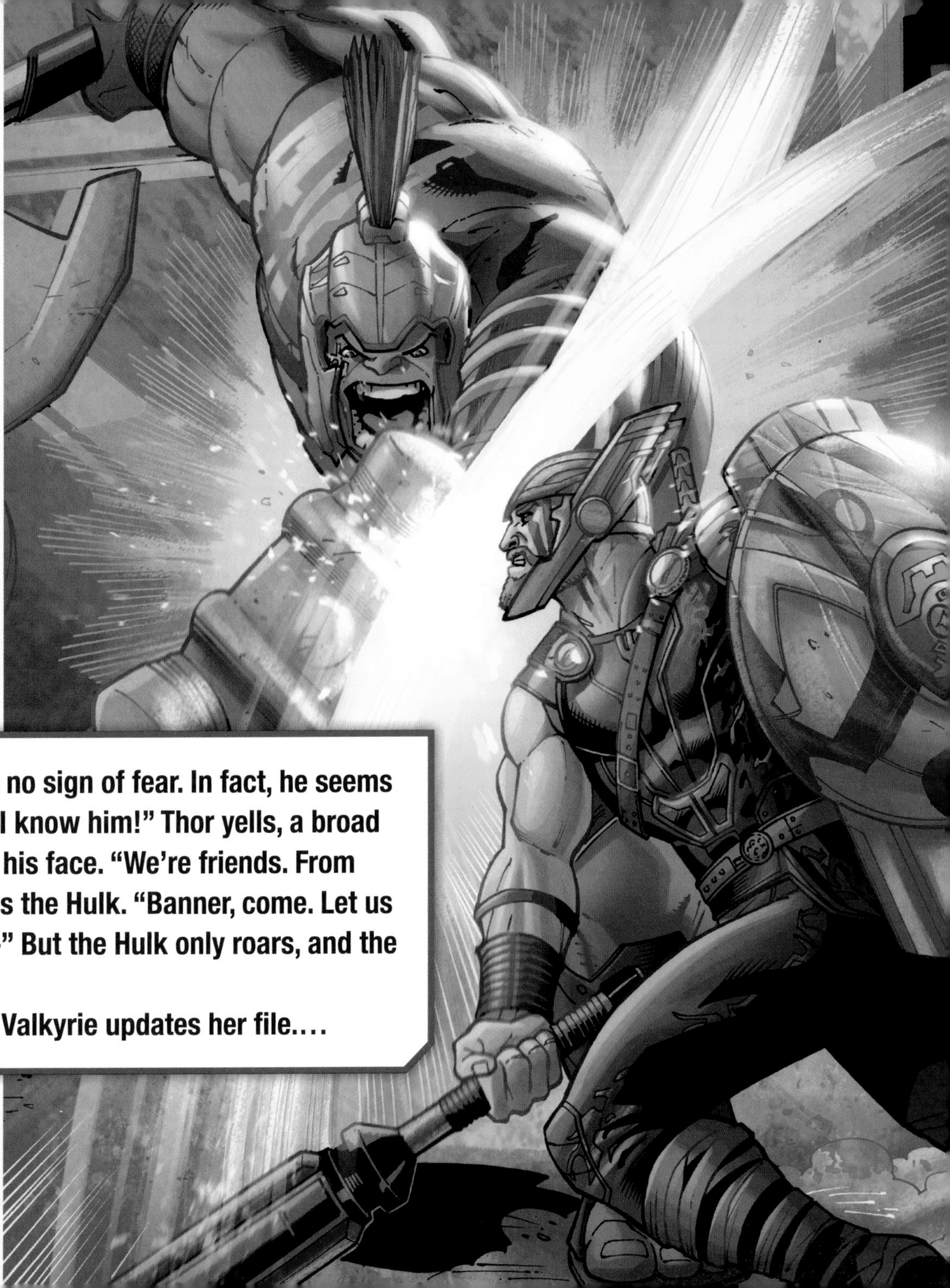

Thor shows no sign of fear. In fact, he seems relieved. "*Yes!* I know him!" Thor yells, a broad smile crossing his face. "We're friends. From work!" He faces the Hulk. "Banner, come. Let us team up and—" But the Hulk only roars, and the battle begins.

Interesting. Valkyrie updates her file. . . .

Accessing Database...

THE HULK

Missing since the Avengers' globe-spanning battle against Ultron, the Hulk's whereabouts are finally uncovered. Reveling in the simplicity of his life as a celebrated Champion, the Hulk is reluctant to return to his former existence. However, a looming threat of universal proportions will force the green Goliath to decide where the Hulk's immense strength is needed most.

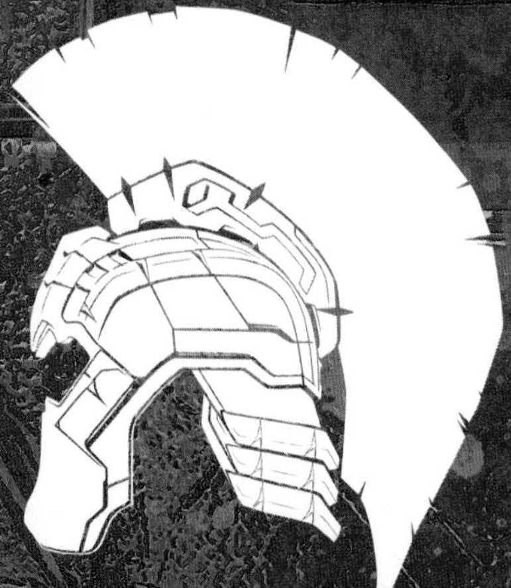

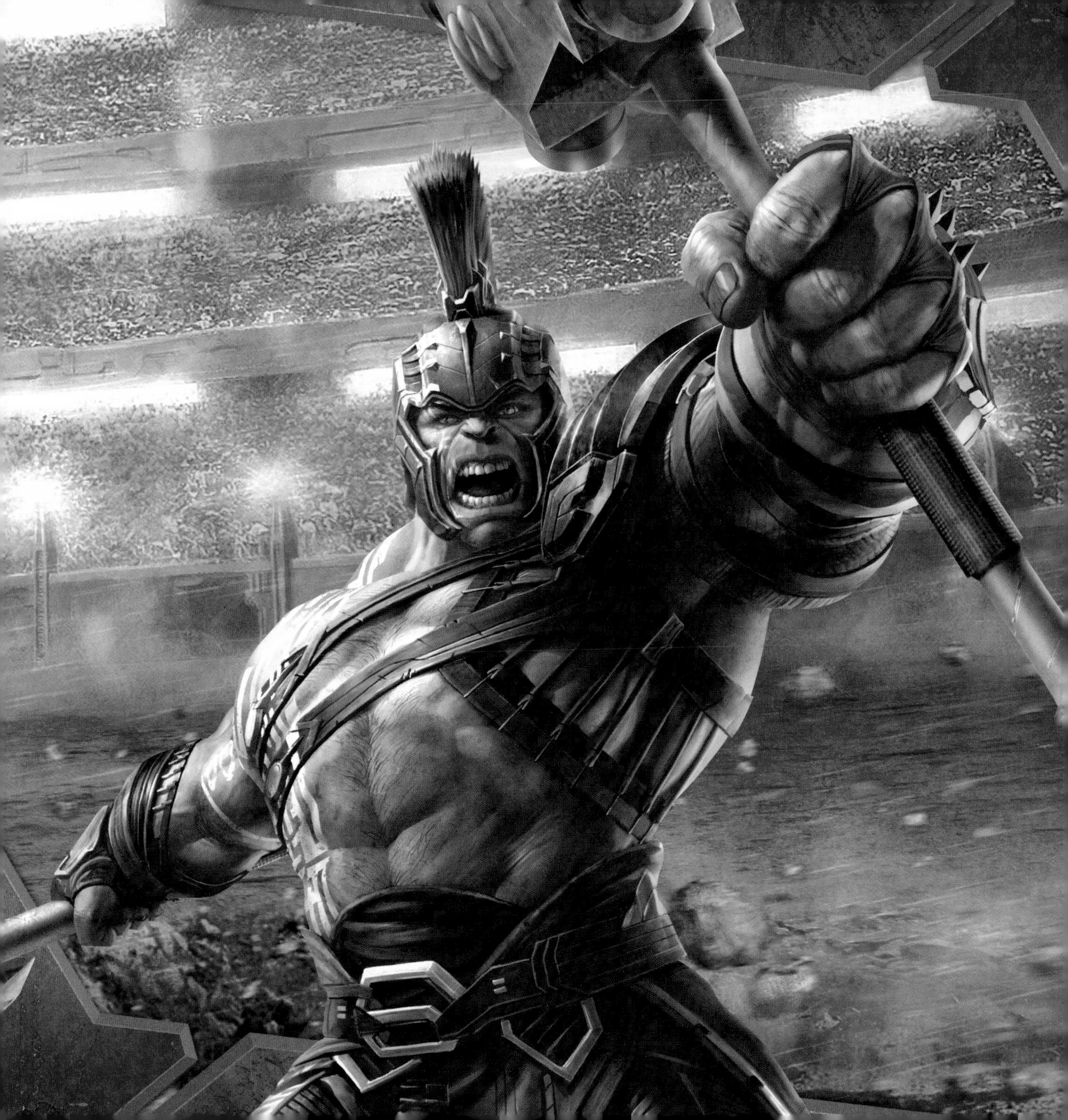

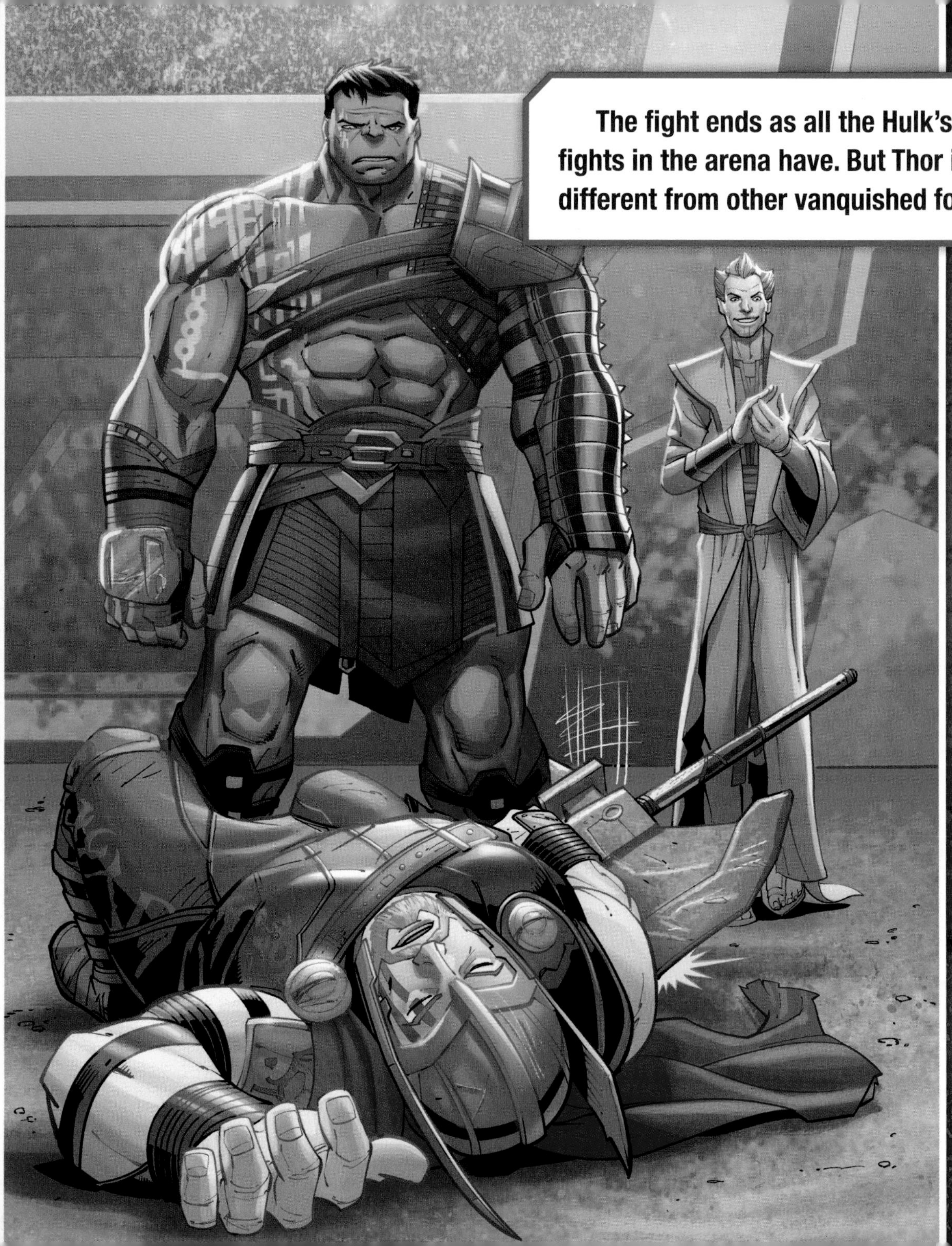
The fight ends as all the Hulk's fights in the arena have. But Thor is different from other vanquished foes.

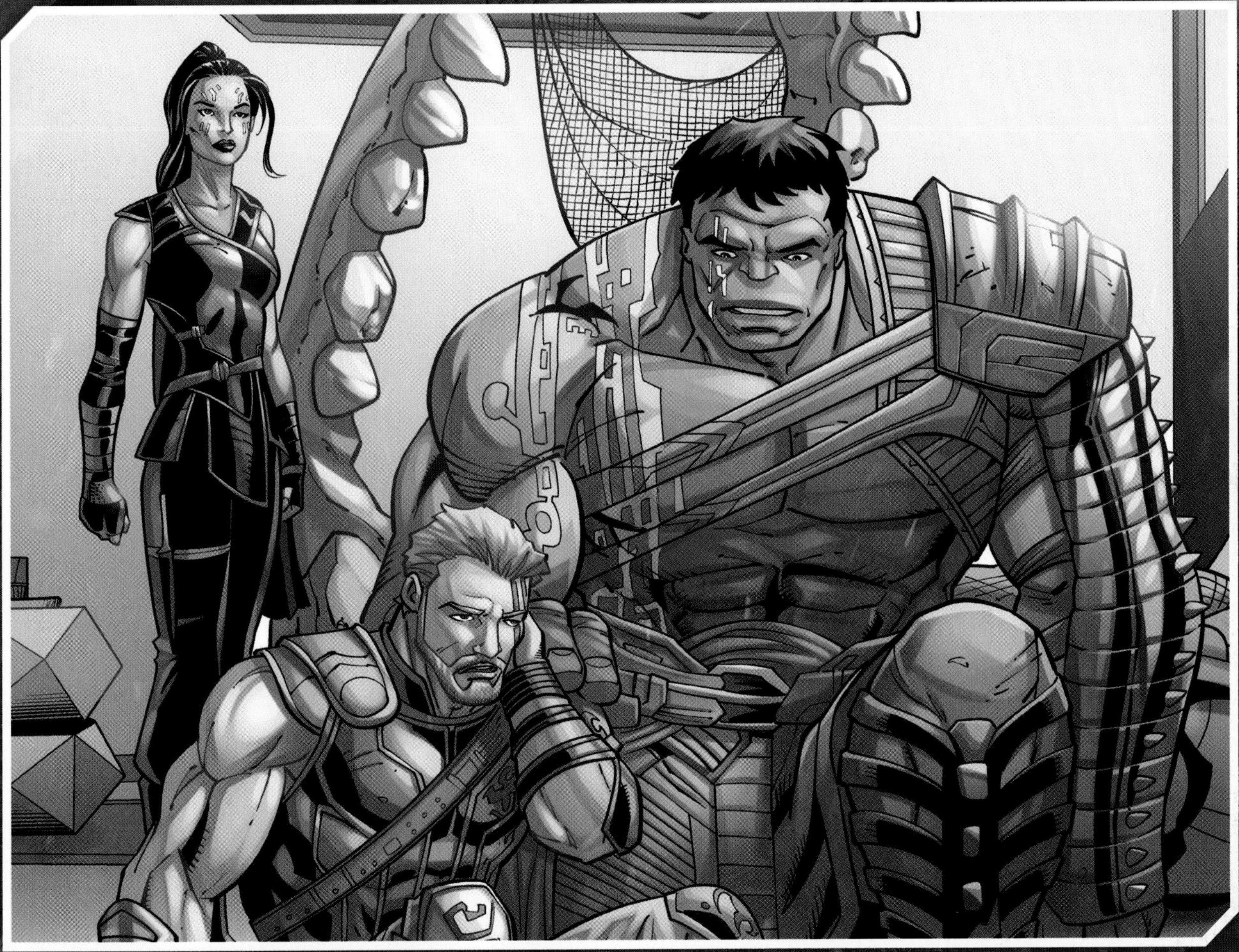

Thor really does know the Hulk, and pleads with both his friend and Valkyrie to help him return home. Asgard needs them all to defeat Hela. They need to find a ship, and Valkyrie searches her records for the perfect one.…

THE *COMMODORE*

This ship is far more than just the Grandmaster's party-vessel. Found on Sakaar, the *Commodore* is equipped to navigate through even the most dangerous cosmic terrain.

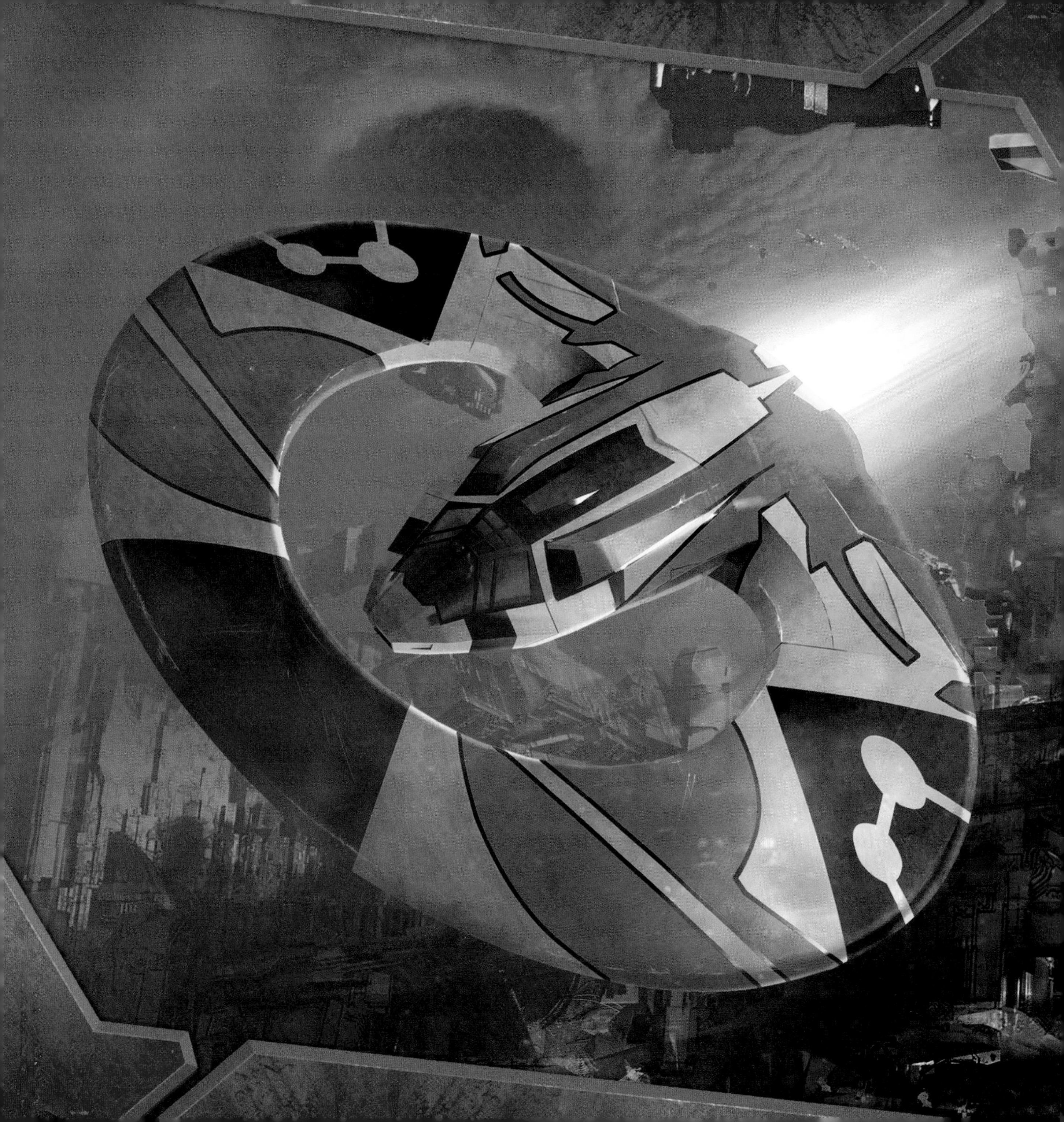

Valkyrie and Thor confirm that the ship really can bring all its occupants through a wormhole and directly to Asgard safely.

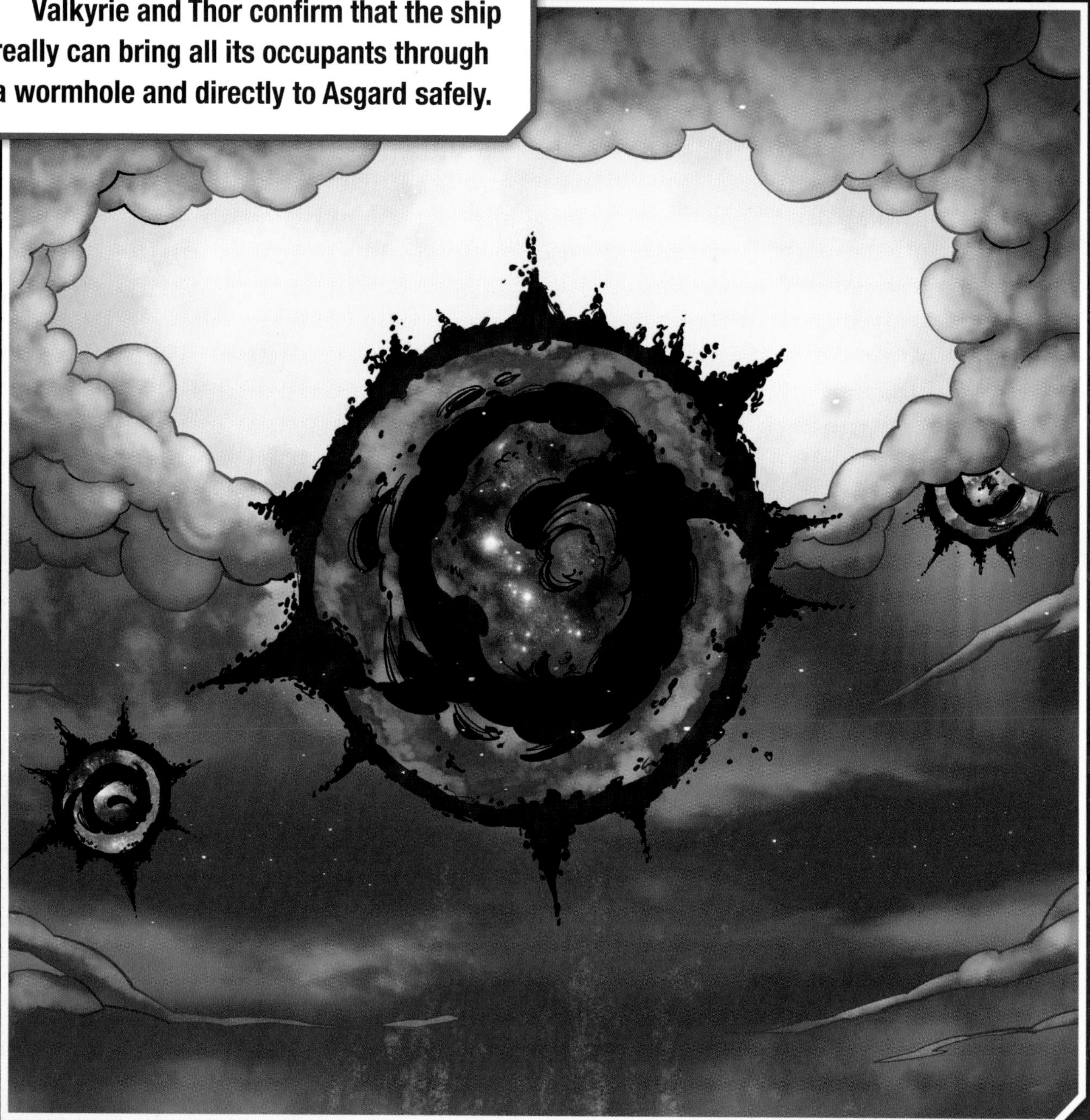

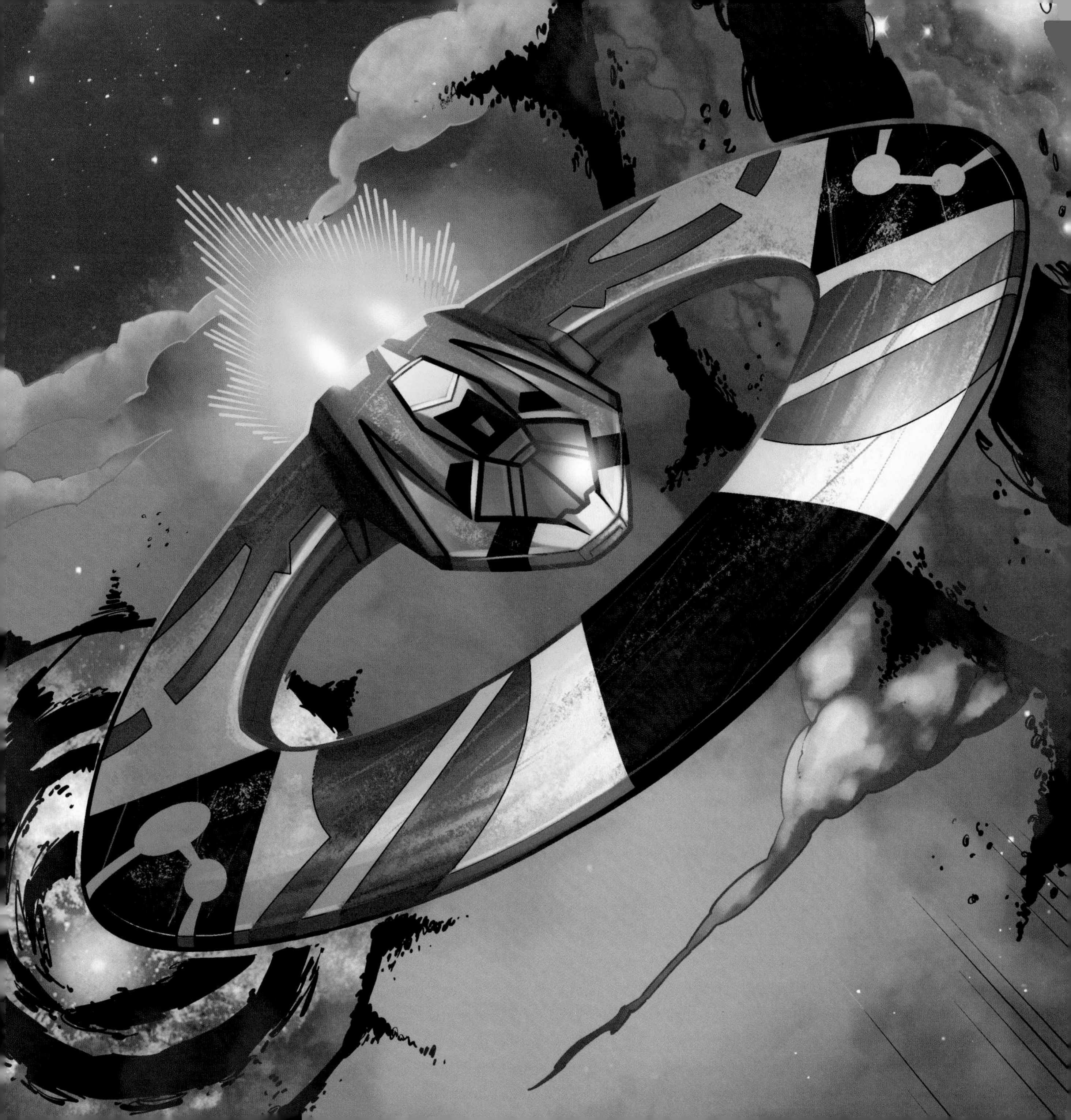

With Thor and the Hulk's genius alter ego, Bruce Banner, in tow, Valkyrie is doing something she never thought she would again: leave. Together with her new allies, she *just* might save Asgard!

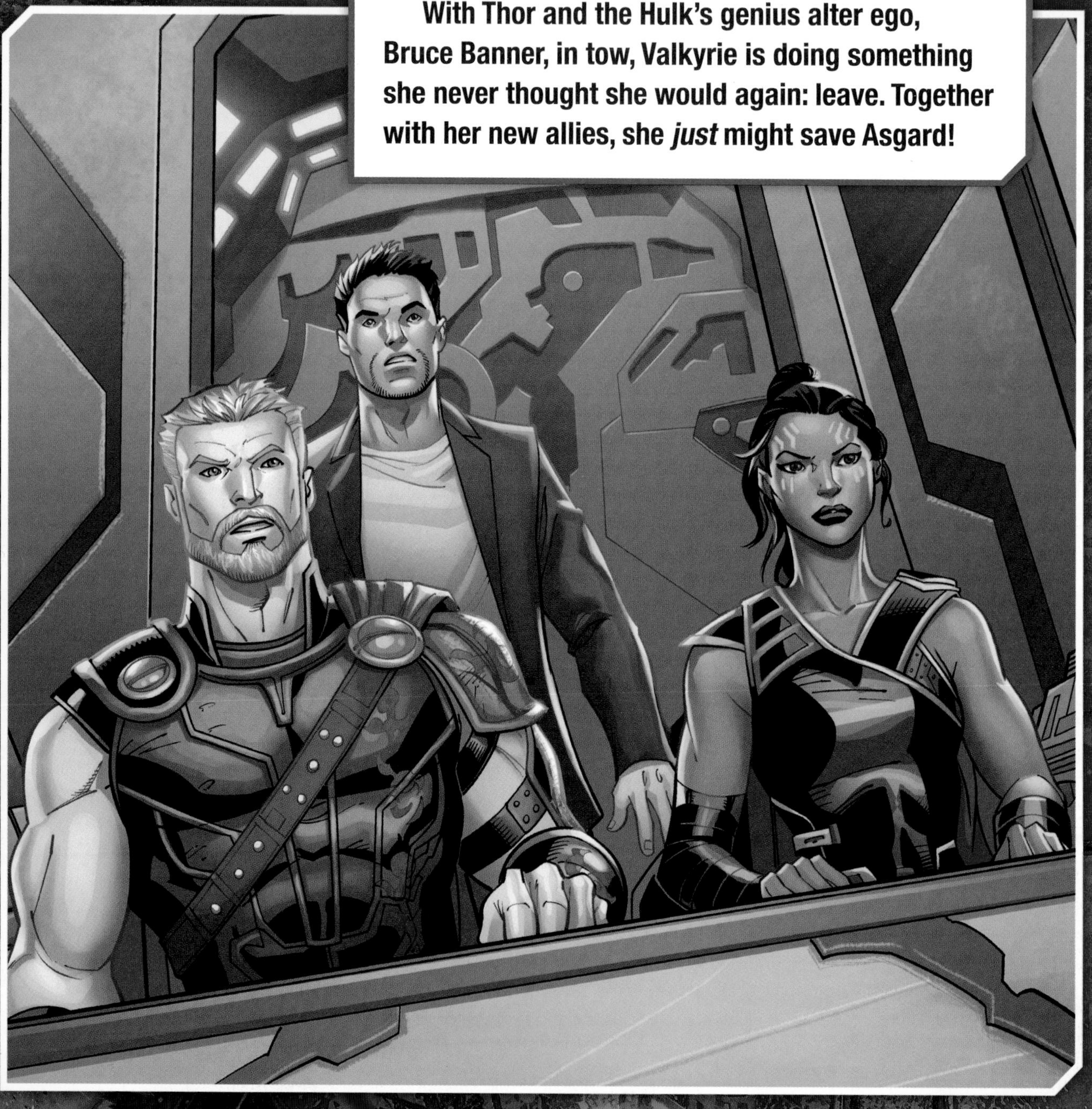